The stable was full that night. All of Bethlehem's visitors had brought horses donkeys and oxen to help carry their families to be counted in the census.

Caesar Augustus, the ruler, told everyone they had to travel back to the place they had been raised, or at least where their family came from, so they could be counted. He wanted to know how many people he ruled.

The Bethlehem Bungalow—a small inn on the edge of town—was full to overflowing.

It was late in the evening when the animals heard the clip-clop of a small donkey's hooves on the cobblestone and mud pavement. He sounded tired, the way he dragged his hooves.

There was a short time of quiet. The animals could hear a man and woman—really a young girl—discussing if they should ask if there was any room for them to sleep. The sign on the door read "No Vacancy: full up due to census."

Sharon the sheep heard the man say, "But Mary, you're going to have a baby. Surely the inn keeper will at least have room for you." Sharon quickly relayed the message to the rest of the animals in the little cave stable—she was a bit of a gossip, especially for a sheep. (Sheep are known to like baa-aaa-aad news, but most of the time they can keep a secret.)

The man knocked on the door. There was no response. He knocked again; still no response.

Finally he beat on the door and hollered, "Is someone in there that can help us?" Dogs barked, a llama snorted and a camel coughed. But there was a dim glow in the Inn.

An elderly man (he was at least 49)
shuffled to the door. He held a candle in
one hand and a club in the other.

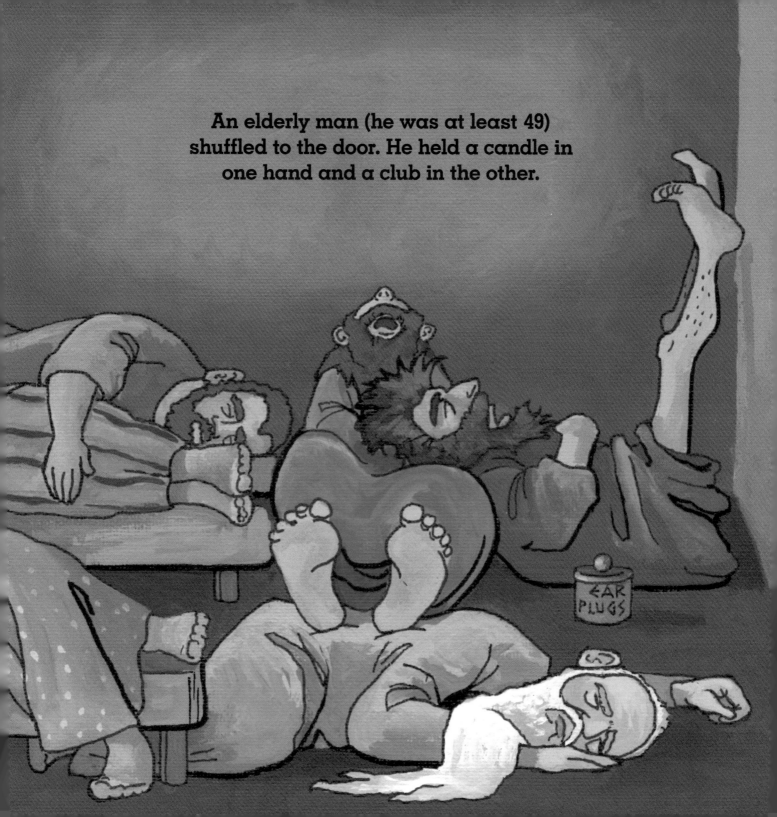

He yelled from inside the inn, "What's the matter? Do you have a problem reading? Read the sign to me and tell me what you think it means! I've been sleeping for two hours and now you wake me from the best sleep I've had in weeks. What do you need? Reading glasses maybe? My stomach feels like I ate too much unleavened bread. Maybe the olive oil was spoiled. Why are you bothering me so late at night anyway?"

The man who knocked apologized and then explained, "My name is Joseph, this is my wife, Mary. She is going to have a baby. Is there someplace we could sleep tonight? I'm worried that the baby could come. My wife has traveled a long way on the back of a donkey—three days we have traveled. The doctor told us it wasn't good timing, but what could we do? The message from Caesar told us we had to come now. Is there someplace we could sleep? Please?"

The innkeeper looked out and saw Mary sitting on the little donkey; she looked so young and tired. "Oh I suppose I could put you up in the stable, but it will cost you, just the same," the innkeeper growled. "Thank you so much," Joseph responded.

Soon the little donkey was munching hay, and Joseph and Mary were snuggled down trying to sleep, even though all the animals in the stable were breathing heavily.

Hank the horse had a snoring problem, and about the time he finally quit, Gertrude the Guernsey cow decided to start chewing her cud.

Clyde the camel kept talking in his sleep. He kept asking a llama named Lewis where the water was and if he had ever heard of a camel named Carmen. After a time though, the animals and the man and woman all drifted off to sleep.

Suddenly, Reuben the rooster was wide-awake. There seemed to be a bright light in the stable.

"Oh no," Reuben thought. "Did I miss it? Has the sun come up and I missed it *again*?" Reuben had been under such stress lately.

Reuben had trouble sleeping. When he finally fell asleep he often slept right through sunrise. Reuben was concerned about his job security.

Reuben looked outside. No,
it was still dark outside; the
sun hadn't come up yet.

Reuben looked back inside the stable. The light was coming from near the manger. There were more people here now too. They looked like shepherds. Yes, they were shepherds. Reuben had seen them before on market day in Bethlehem. They would walk through the streets and sell wool and yarn.

The shepherds were on their knees. They seemed to be worshipping the little bundle in the manger. It was a baby. The girl—Mary—said the baby's name was Jesus.

The shepherds were talking about how they had been told by angels that all this had happened. They were telling how angels had appeared and said to them,

*"Glory to God in the highest heaven,
and peace on earth to all whom God favors." (Luke 2:14)*

After a short while, the shepherds left. They went out and told anyone who would listen about this baby Jesus that had been born in a stable in Bethlehem.

Reuben couldn't wait to tell others
about what he had seen as well.
He looked forward to waking up
the town of Bethlehem at daybreak.

No, Reuben wouldn't miss the sun coming up the next morning. He wouldn't sleep anymore this night. Reuben wanted to make sure he could crow at the first sign of light on that first Christmas morning. Crowing would be Reuben's way of celebrating Jesus' birth.

God wants each of us to celebrate the birth of his son Jesus, just like the roosters celebrate the coming up of the sun.

God loved us so much that he was willing to send his son to be born in a stable so we could live with him again in heaven some day. We just need to believe that Jesus died for us on the cross.

God has given us a great gift. He came wrapped in blankets instead of paper. And just like the shepherds, we need to tell others what we have heard about this little baby that was born in a stable in Bethlehem.

When the sun finally rose on that first Christmas
morning Reuben celebrated God's gift to the
world with his first Christmas crow.

CPSIA information can be obtained
at www.ICGtesting.com
Printed in the USA
LVIW010711140712
290084LV00001B